KUMAK'S FISH

A Tall Tale FROM THE Far North

MICHAEL BANIA

On a beautiful Arctic morning,
Kumak looked out the window of his house.
Through the willows he could see the sun rising over the frozen river.

"Ahhh, spring," said Kumak to his family.
"The days are long. The nights are short, and the ice is still hard.
Good day for fish."

"*Good day for fish,*"
said Kumak's wife,
pulling on her
warm parka.

"*Good day for fish,*"
said his wife's mother,
pulling on her
warm mukluks.

"*Good day for fish,*"
said his sons and daughters,
pulling on their warm beaver hats
and fur-lined gloves.

Kumak packed his fishing gear on his sled.

He packed his wife on the sled.

He packed his wife's mother on the sled.

He packed his sons and daughters on the sled.

And then, in the safest place of all,

Kumak packed his Uncle Aglu's amazing hooking stick.

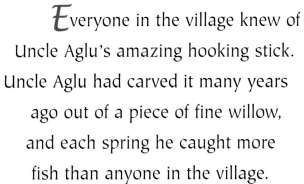

Everyone in the village knew of
Uncle Aglu's amazing hooking stick.
Uncle Aglu had carved it many years
ago out of a piece of fine willow,
and each spring he caught more
fish than anyone in the village.

But this spring,
Uncle Aglu's legs were stiff.
He told Kumak to use
the amazing hooking stick.

This was Kumak's lucky day!

When they reached the great, frozen lake past the mouth of the river,
Kumak's family dug their fishing holes and sat down to wait.

Kumak and his family sat for a long time.

They were quiet. They were patient.

They scooped away the ice growing around their fishing holes.

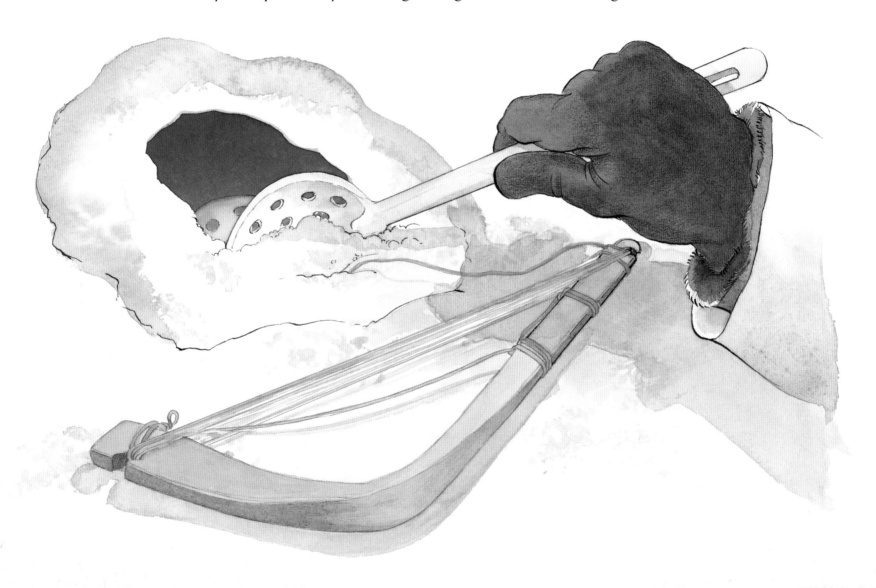

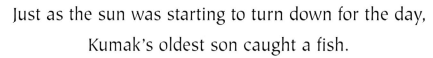

Just as the sun was starting to turn down for the day,
Kumak's oldest son caught a fish.
Then Kumak's two daughters
each caught a fish.

Soon his wife and
his wife's mother each caught a fish.
"Good day for fish!" they said.

Kumak was quiet.
He was patient.
He scooped away the ice
growing around his fishing hole.

Suddenly, Uncle Aglu's amazing hooking stick began to twitch.

It twitched this way.

It twitched that way.

It went around and around.

It gave one more twitch,

then yanked Kumak toward the fishing hole.

"What a big fish!" said Kumak's wife.

"Biggest I can remember!" said his wife's mother.

"The biggest fish ever!" said his sons and daughters.

They danced with joy, thinking about the happy faces
of the villagers when they brought the fish home.

Just then, Kumak began to twitch.

He twitched this way.

He twitched that way.

He went around and around.

Kumak gave one more twitch
and slid headfirst
toward the fishing hole and the icy water below.

"Wife! Help me pull this fish!"

Kumak's wife grabbed him around the waist and together they took two steps back.

"That fish must be as big as a seal!" yelled Kumak happily.

"Aana! Help me pull this fish!" His wife's mother ran to help.

She took hold of Kumak's wife and together they took three steps back.

"That fish must be as big as a walrus!" yelled Kumak happily.

"Children! Help me pull this fish!" His sons and daughters ran to help.

They lined up, one behind the other, and never let go.

Together they took six more steps,

but the stick pulled them all the way back to the edge of the hole.

"That fish must be as big as a whale!" yelled Kumak happily.
Villagers on their way home heard Kumak's shouts and ran to help.
They lined up behind Kumak's family and
holding on tight to the person in front of them,
they pulled and pulled.
But no matter how many steps they took away from the hole,
they always ended up back where they started.

Soon the whole village heard about Kumak's fish and came to help.
In one long line stretching across the frozen lake,
they pulled and pulled
and **PULLED!**

Once again, Uncle Aglu's amazing hooking stick began to twitch. It twitched this way, and all the people of the village twitched this way.

It twitched that way,
and all the people of the village
twitched that way.

It went around and around, and all the people of the village went around and around.

Uncle Aglu's amazing hooking stick
gave one more enormous twitch
and pulled Kumak down the fishing hole
and into the icy water below!

Kumak's family and the villagers didn't give up.
Each person held on tight to the person in front of them
and never let go.
All together, they gave one more mighty pull and . . .

WHOOSH!

Kumak came flying
back out of the fishing hole.
Uncle Aglu's amazing hooking stick
came flying out with him.

Stretched out in one long line,
all around Kumak and the fishing hole, were hundreds of fish!
Each fish held on tight to the one in front of it and never let go.
Kumak had landed enough fish
for the entire village to have a splendid feast.

"Hooray for Kumak!" cheered the villagers as they picked up the fish.

"Hooray for Uncle Aglu's amazing hooking stick!" said Kumak as they started home.

It was a good day for fish.

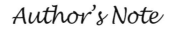

Author's Note

Kumak = KOO-muk   Aglu = AH-gloo

Many years ago, after feeding in a shallow bay, a young whale mistakenly turned into the mouth of the Buckland River instead of heading out to sea off the coast of Northwest Alaska. Two Iñupiat men, hunting on the river for moose, were astonished when they saw the whale swimming up the river. They harpooned the whale but were unable to pull it ashore. Darkness came upon them and they returned to the village of Buckland, where word of their great fortune spread. The next morning, all able-bodied men and women launched their boats and rode twenty miles down the river to help.

Coincidentally, this was a special day at the school. It was "Iñupiaq Day," when parents and elders come and demonstrate traditional customs for the children. Stories of the old ways are shared, traditional foods are prepared, and skills of Iñupiaq life are taught. Students often take field trips to learn things like how to set snares or hook fish, but on this very special day the children were invited to help with the whale!

When everyone reached the spot where the whale lay in the river, excitement filled the air. For many this was a once-in-a-lifetime event. They tied a rope around the tail of the whale and everyone, big and small, took hold, lining up one behind the other. Upon a signal from the leaders, they pulled and pulled. After many tries, the villagers finally pulled the whale out of the water.

I watched this amazing tug-of-war from the sky as I flew overhead in a small plane, and the image inspired the idea for *Kumak's Fish*. On that wonderful day, the whale was butchered and shared equally with each family in the village. Kumak did the same with the fish from Uncle Aglu's amazing hooking stick.

Thanks to the Iñupiaq values of cooperation, sharing, and humor, each story had a happy ending and the village succeeded. These were, indeed, good days for all.

**To the men and women of the NANA region who dedicate their lives
to keeping the ways of their ancestors alive.**

Special thanks to Dianne, for a special gift, and to Isiq, for making Uncle Aglu's amazing hooking stick. Taikuu!

Library of Congress Cataloging-in-Publication Data
available on request

Hardbound ISBN 0-88240-583-7
Softbound ISBN 0-88240-584-5

President: Charles M. Hopkins
Associate Publisher: Douglas A. Pfeiffer
Editorial Staff: Timothy W. Frew,
    Tricia Brown, Kathy Howard,
    Jean Andrews, Jean Bond-Slaughter
Production Staff: Richard L. Owsiany,
    Susan Dupere
Editor: Michelle McCann
Designer: Constance Bollen, cb graphics

Printed in Hong Kong

Alaska Northwest Books®
An imprint of Graphic Arts Center Publishing Company
P.O. Box 10306, Portland, Oregon 97296-0306 • 503-226-2402; www.gacpc.com